Why Cowboys Need a Pardner

Why Cowboys Need a Pardner

By Laurie Lazzaro Knowlton

Illustrated by James Rice

PELICAN PUBLISHING COMPANY
Gretna 1998

Love never fails. (1 Cor. 13:8)

To my Creator in thanksgiving for my pardner, Tom

Library of Congress Cataloging-in-Publication Data

Knowlton, Laurie Lazzaro.
    Why cowboys need a pardner / by Laurie Lazzaro Knowlton ;
illustrated by James Rice.
        p. cm.
    Summary: Alone on the range, cowboy Slim Jim Watkins meets a Pony
Express rider returning a mail order bride and finds himself a
pardner with whom he can share conversation.
    ISBN 1-56554-336-X (hardcover : alk. paper)
    [1. Cowboys—Fiction. 2. Pony express—Fiction. 3. Mail order
brides—Fiction. 4. West (U.S.)—Fiction.] I. Rice, James, 1934-
ill. II. Title.
PZ7.K7685Wg 1998
[Fic]—DC21   98-19956
                                                                CIP
                                                                AC

Printed in Hong Kong

Published by Pelican Publishing Company, Inc.
P.O. Box 3110, Gretna, Louisiana 70054-3110

WHY COWBOYS NEED A PARDNER

Slim Jim Watkins was one lonesome cowboy. It was just him and his horse Bonecrusher riding the range. Why, he was so hungry for conversation that he began hearing the cattle talk. But that didn't help him much. He was gonna have t' hire himself a wrangler.

So Slim Jim Watkins headed for the nearest town. No sooner did he arrive than he noticed things looked a might peculiar.

Slim Jim Watkins peered inside each doorway. There was no one, not even a greenhorn.

"There's no butcher, no baker, no sarsaparilla maker!" said Slim Jim Watkins.

"Guess it's just you and me, fella. Bonecrusher, did I ever tell you about the time Bull-faced Billy bounced off his bronco?"

Bonecrusher gave a snort and they were off.

Slim Jim Watkins was one lonesome cowboy.

Not far out of town, Slim Jim Watkins came across a moss-horned old timer picking a stone out of his horse's hoof.

"Well, howdy, pardner!" Slim Jim Watkins called. "I was beginning to think I was the only human being this side of the Mississippi!"

"Yep." The old-timer never looked up.

"It gets a might lonesome out here with no one to talk to."

"Yep." The old-timer climbed on his horse.

"Been looking for a wrangler to come work my spread and engage in a little conversation." Slim Jim Watkins, hoping, cocked his head.

"Nope," said that moss-horned old-timer.

"I'd say that's a man of few words," said Slim Jim Watkins.

Slim Jim Watkins nudged his horse. "Bonecrusher, did I ever tell you 'bout the time Auntie May got her skirt caught in the windmill?"

Bonecrusher gave a snort and they were off.

Slim Jim Watkins was one lonesome cowboy. He rode 'til he spied a cloud of dust on the horizon. Why, that cloud was traveling faster than a tumbleweed in a tornado!

"Howdy, pardner! What's the rush?" Slim Jim Watkins pulled alongside the rider.

"Got myself some delicate cargo I need to return. The mail must get through," said the rider.

Slim Jim Watkins looked from the Pony Express rider to the gal behind him. "Did you say return?"

"She's a mail-order bride. When I delivered her to the groom, he was six feet under."

The gal dropped the rope over the Pony Express rider.

"Now don't start that again, missy!" The Pony Express rider moaned. "You ain't got a groom, so this is a 'return to sender' if'n I ever saw one."

Well, Slim Jim Watkins gave that gal a second look. She wasn't a wrangler, but she could be someone to carry on a conversation with and she was good with a rope.

"I know I'm not your intended, but I've been lookin' for a wrangler to he'p with my spread down San Antone' way. And I'd be much obliged for a little conversation." Slim gave his most handsome smile.

The Pony Express man shook his finger. "Nope, nope, nope! That's against regulations. All mail must be delivered to its proper party or returned to sender—Code number 630."

That gal crossed her arms. "Was that a proposal? 'Cuz I won't be taken for granted. I came lookin' for a man to call my own . . ."

But before that gal could finish, the Pony Express rider gave his horse a kick and they were off.

Watching the two ride away, Slim got to feeling lonelier than a skunk on a Sunday stroll.

Yep, Slim Jim Watkins was one lonesome cowboy. "Mail-order brides. Maybe I should send away for one of them gals?" Slim Jim Watkins gave Bonecrusher a nudge.

"Did I ever tell you about the time the preacher hitched a feller..."

Suddenly Slim Jim Watkins had himself a right bright idea.
"Come on, Bonecrusher! We have some fast talking to do."
Bonecrusher gave a snort and they were off.

"Excuse me, sir. May I ask the lady a question?" Slim inquired.
The Pony Express man just kept riding.
"Miss, can you tell me who your sender is?" Slim asked.
The gal smiled. "Why, I am, sir."

The Pony Express rider pulled up on the reins. He looked from the gal to Slim. "If you are the sender, then this delivery is complete."

"Well, I'll be hitched!" said Slim. "I got myself a mail-order bride!"

"Well, yahoo!" said the gal. "You got yourself a pardner."

"Let's go find ourselves a preacher," said Slim.

Then that gal climbed on Bonecrusher and before Slim Jim Watkins could say a word, that gal got to talking faster than Slim Jim Watkins could listen.

Bonecrusher gave a snort and they were off.